Saily's Journey

By Ralph da Costa Nunez

with Karina Kwok

Illustrated by Madeline Gerstein Simon

White Tiger Press

New York

Published in the United States by:
White Tiger Press
521 West 49th Street
New York, NY 10019
212-529-5252

Printed in the United States of America

Introduction

In all the years that I have been involved with homelessness, it is the children that have had the most profound effect on me. While the resilience and hope of youth are visible in their faces, the reality of homelessness is undeniable. Their dreams for the future are in jeopardy, replaced by fear and anxiety. Their belief in themselves waivers, replaced by skepticism. Their innocence is lost, replaced by adult burdens. And the longer they are homeless, the worse it becomes.

But this can change. The beginning of the end of homelessness starts with children themselves. By educating today's youth to the fact that the fastest growing segment of the homeless population are children, we can create an awareness that can help us turn the corner on this American tragedy. And by spreading their awareness to their teachers and parents, we can build an army of support.

In this children's book, Saily the Snail experiences despair and hope on his journey to find a new home. But his encounters with friends and foes along the way offer lessons about homelessness for children and adults alike. We must make it our responsibility to increase a national awareness of the harsh realities that so many of these children face every day. In doing so, we become united in an effort to guarantee that no child in America is without a home.

Leonard N. Stern
Founder/Chairman
Homes for the Homeless
New York City

"Can you tell us the story about the dragons today?"

"A scary story! One with ghosts!"

"No! A fairy tale about a princess!"

Miss Kate smiled. "Come sit on the floor around me. I have a special story for you," she told the class.
When everyone quieted down, Miss Kate began to tell her tale.

Once upon a time, there was a green polka-dotted snail named Saily who loved the water. Every day after school, Saily ran to the pond, jumped on his sailboat, and let the wind push him about.

Saily loved to dream of the places he would travel to one day.

One afternoon, when Saily was out on his boat, black clouds appeared in the sky and darkness came over the pond. A flash of lightning lit up the sky, and....

10

BOOM!

BOOM!

Thunder shook the air.

It was so dark and windy.

Saily was scared.

He tried hard to hold onto his boat, but...

BOOM, BOOM, BOOM!

That was all Saily could remember when he woke up on the beach.

His smashed boat lay on the sand. And next to him lay broken pieces of what looked like his shell.

"Oh no!" Saily cried, his eyes filled with tears.
"My shell is broken. Now what will I do?
My shell is my home. Without it I have
nowhere to live."

Saily picked himself up and slowly wiggled away from the pond.

Soon Saily passed by a snail family.
The youngest began to point and giggle. "Look mom! That snail has no shell! He looks different. Where does he live?"
The mother snail pulled her children close to protect them from Saily.

"I don't understand," thought Saily sadly. "Why are they making fun of me? Is it because I don't have a home?"

The sky turned orange and red as the sun set. Saily knew he had to find a home soon, or else he would have to sleep outside. But then he saw something down the path.

Right in the middle of the path was a peanut shell!

"Perfect!" Saily thought. "This will fit me just fine."

Saily nudged the shell with his head and crawled underneath.

"It's dark in here!" "It's dark in here!" "It's dark in here"

The peanut shell echoed Saily's voice. "This won't do, this won't do, this won't do."

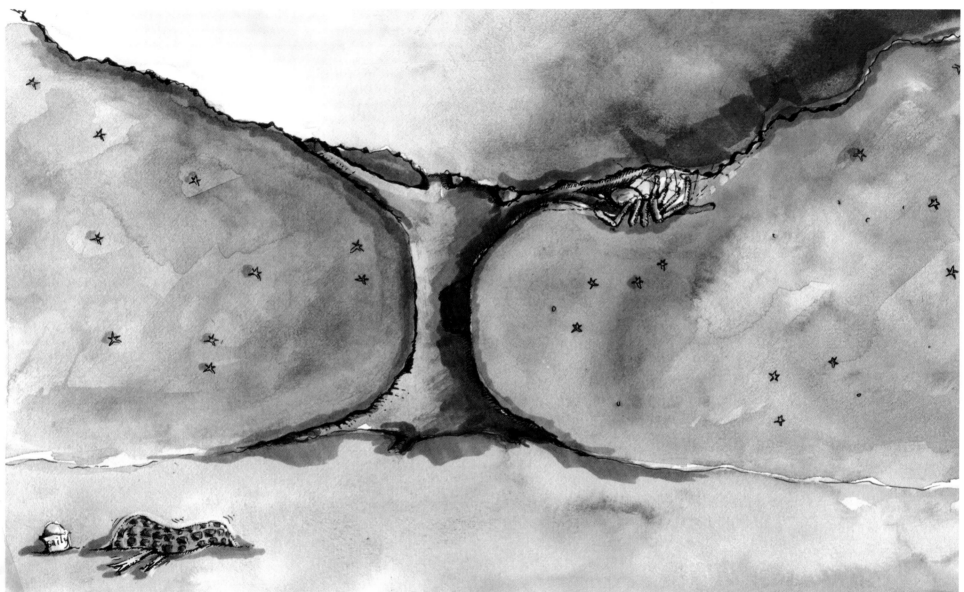

Meanwhile from a nearby tree, a spider was watching Saily.

She was very, very hungry.

Saily peeked out of his peanut shell. "Oh gosh! This might be good for a peanut, but it won't ever do for a snail!"

"*Yoo hoo*!"
the spider called.

Saily looked to the right...
Then he looked to the left...

And then he
turned in a circle.
He could not see who
was calling him, and he was
getting very dizzy.

"Yoo hoo, up here!"

"My name," the spider said, "is Jasmine!"
Just then Saily's stomach began to rumble. He was starting to get hungry.
Jasmine licked her lips. "I'm going to get something to eat. If you are hungry, you
may come along."

Jasmine dropped to the ground from the tree and began to walk through the woods with Saily following her.

"Psst! Hey you!"

Saily turned around and was face to face with a cricket wearing a black bandanna.

"Whoa... Who are you?" asked Saily.

"Shh!" The cricket looked around. "I'm here to help you!"

"Help me to do what?"

"She wants to eat you for dinner! RUN FOR YOUR LIFE!" the cricket yelled.

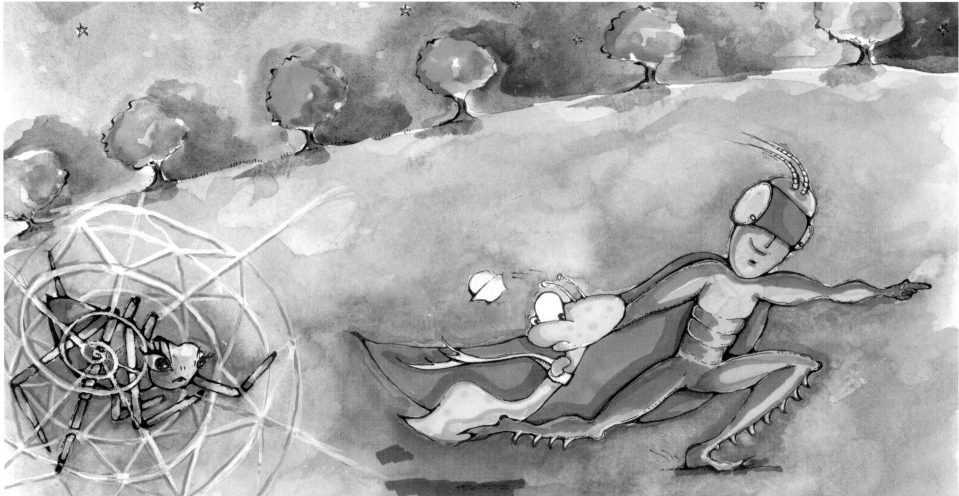

As Jasmine spun around, the cricket grabbed Saily by the hand and they ran with the spider close behind them.

"You are not getting away from me!" Jasmine yelled.

Saily and the cricket leapt and jumped through the trees when all the sudden...

"ARGHH!!!"

Jasmine was stuck in another spider's web! "I'll get you someday!" she yelled.

When they reached the road, Saily and the cricket stopped to catch their breath. "ARE YOU CRAZY?" the cricket yelled. "YOU COULD HAVE BEEN EATEN ALIVE! JASMINE IS THE MOST FEARED SPIDER OF THE FOREST!" Saily looked down at the ground. "Thank you for helping me. I was in a storm, and my shell broke. Now I don't have a home."

23

"Are you homeless?" asked the cricket.

"Homeless? What's that?" asked Saily.

"Homeless means you don't have a place to live," explained the cricket.

"Then I guess I'm homeless," said Saily.

"Don't worry," said the cricket. My name's Clark, and you can stay with my family until you find another shell."

When they reached Clark's home, there were crickets everywhere! They were all rubbing their wings together amd making lots of noise.

"Here we are in Cricket House! Mom, Dad, this is my friend Saily. His shell broke in a storm, so he doesn't have a home. Can he sleep over tonight?" asked Clark.

"Of course!" they all said. "Come and make yourself at home, Saily."

Clark showed Saily to a spare bed. But Saily could not sleep because...

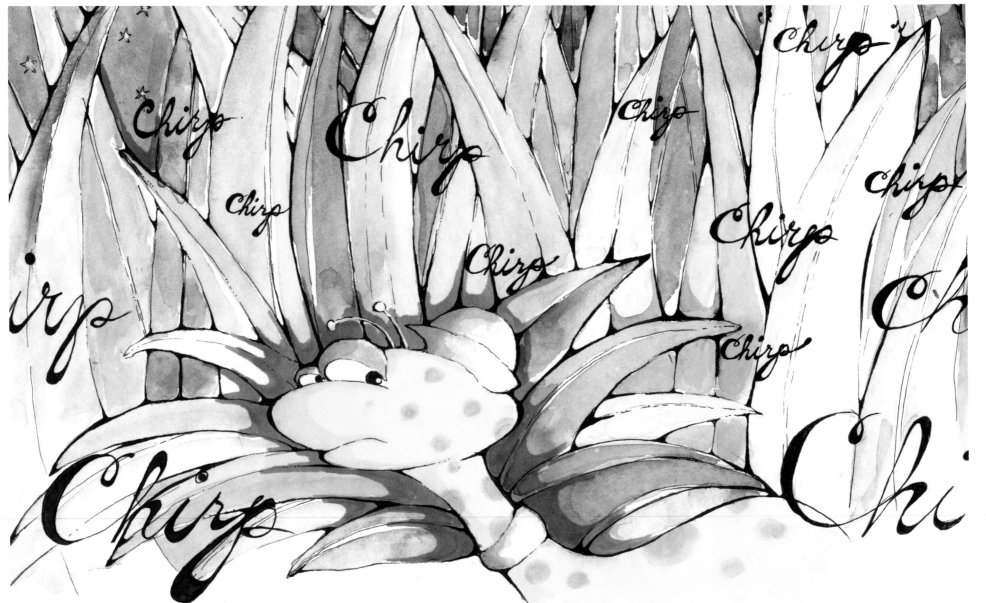

Little chirps, big chirps, all kinds of chirps... ALL NIGHT LONG! Boy, it was noisy! Saily didn't sleep a wink.

When the sun came up, Clark was already awake. "Hey Saily!" he called out. "What are you doing today?"

"I need to find a home of my own. I can't stay here forever," Saily said.

Clark looked puzzled. "Where do you want to go?"

"I think I'll go back to the pond. Maybe I'll find something there."

"What's it like, you know, not having a home?" Clark asked.

"Oh, it's very lonely. Other animals treat me like
I'm different and they look at me funny. Sometimes
they point. Sometimes they laugh."

"I don't think you are different. I think you are a great friend."

Saily's eyes brimmed with tears. "Thank you," he said.

"Well, good luck Saily. I hope you find
a home, but remember - you're
always welcome here!"

Saily went on his way and walked for hours. He felt very lonely. "Being homeless is scary," Saily thought to himself. "I miss sailing on my boat."

Then, all of the sudden, Saily found himself face to face with the strangest looking bird he had ever seen!"

"What are you?" asked Saily.

"I'm a seagull! My name is Charlie."

"I've never seen a seagull! Where do you live?" asked Saily.

"I live by the ocean!" said Charlie.

"What does the ocean look like?" asked Saily.

"Come, I'll show you! Hop on my back, we're going for a ride!"

30

Up
Up
And
Away!

Higher and higher they flew until Saily could see what he thought was a large pond, the largest pond he had ever seen!
"That's the ocean!" Charlie said. "Lots of fish live there. It's their home."

Charlie flew lower and lower and closer and closer to the ocean. Suddenly, Saily yelled, "Look! Stop, stop! Look down there!"
Charlie landed on the beach in the middle of all kinds of shells.

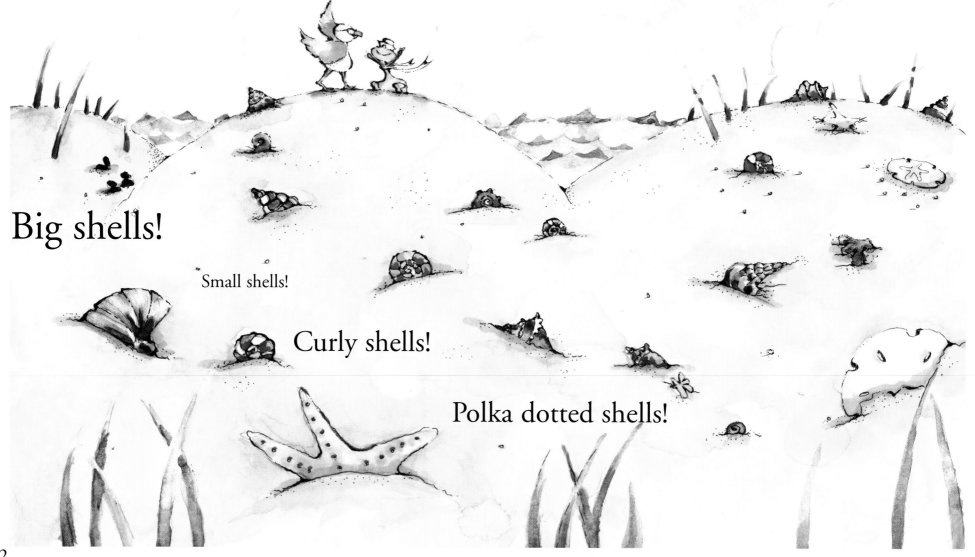

Big shells!

Small shells!

Curly shells!

Polka dotted shells!

Saily started to try on shells until he found a perfect, polka-dotted one!
"I have a home again!" Saily said. "It's perfect!"

"Hey Saily!" Charlie shouted. "Here's some wood! We can build you a new boat!"

That afternoon, Saily and Charlie built a new boat. Soon, Saily was sailing again and back to the place where he belonged. He was home.

"Did you know that children could be homeless too?" asked Miss Kate.
Jamal spoke up. "It's not just snails that are homeless?"
"It must be pretty scary not having a home," said Sophie.

"Homeless children are not any different than you and other children you know," Miss Kate explained.

The students looked at their teacher. "I wish no one was ever homeless," Jamal said.

"Saily was able to find a new home with help from his friends. Can you think of anything we can do to help homeless children?" asked Miss Kate.

mnoPqrstuvwxYz

"We can collect food for them!" said Tamika.

"How about donating clothes?" asked Vanessa.

"We can treat all children the same and not tease them if they are homeless," offered Carlos.

Miss Kate smiled at her students. "That, Carlos, is probably the most important message of all."

Did you know that the typical homeless person in America is a child ?

Now you do. Want to help?

For more information about family homelessness and what you can do to help, contact:
Homes for the Homeless • New York City • 212-529-5252 • www.homesforthehomeless.com